LOUDMOUTH
George and the Fishing Trip

LOUDMOUTH
George *and the* Fishing Trip

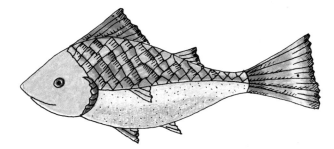

Nancy Carlson

Carolrhoda Books, Inc. ♦ Minneapolis

to Maddie Simons
because of her encouragement and energy

LIBRARY OF CONGRESS CATALOGING IN PUBLICATION DATA

Carlson, Nancy L.
  Loudmouth George and the fishing trip.

  Summary: Loudmouth George, a rabbit who brags about
catching the biggest fish even though he had never been
fishing, is embarrassed by the size of the fish he
finally does catch.
  [1. Rabbits—Fiction. 2. Animals—Fiction.
3. Fishing—Fiction. 4. Pride and vanity—Fiction.]
I. Title.
PZ7.C21665Lo 1983   [E]   82-22159
ISBN 0-87614-213-7

  3   4   5   6   7   8   9   10   92   91   90   89   88   87   86   85

George was always bragging.

According to him, he ran the fastest,

and he ate the biggest pizzas,

and he read the thickest books.

So when Harriet told him she was going
fishing on Saturday, of course George
bragged that he caught the biggest fish.

"If you're such a good fisherman," said
Harriet, "why don't you come with us?"

"I'd better not," said George. "I'd probably
catch such a big fish, it would sink the boat."

Harriet didn't believe him for a minute. When she got home, she asked her dad if George could come with them on Saturday.

"Sure," said Dad. "I'll give his parents a call."

"Guess what, George?" said George's
mother. "Harriet's father just called and
invited you to go fishing tomorrow. Won't
that be fun?"

Oh, no! thought George. Why did I brag so much? The biggest fish I ever caught was in the pet shop.

Early the next morning they were off to the river.

"George, I brought an extra fishing rod if you need it," said Harriet's mother.

"As a matter of fact, I do. You see, the last time I went fishing, I hooked this enormous fish. It was so big, it broke my fishing rod," George bragged.

At last they were out on the water.

"Here's a worm for your hook, George,"
said Harriet.

"I thought you'd fished before," said Harriet.

"Well, I have," George fibbed, "but we didn't use worms. We used other stuff."

So Harriet baited George's hook. Then they
sat ... and they sat ...

. . . and they sat. They sat for three hours, and no one got even a nibble.

"I think we'll call it a day," said Harriet's
father. "The fish just aren't biting today."

Thank heaven, thought George as he started to reel in his line. Suddenly his bobber went down.

"You've got a fish, George!" yelled Harriet.

"Oh, wow!" said George. "Help! What do
I do?"

"I thought you were the great fisherman,"
said Harriet.

"Uh...uh...I guess I exaggerated a little
bit," George confessed. "Help me!"

"Keep reeling it in, George," Harriet told
him.

"It's the biggest fish ever!" yelled George.

"You almost have it, George," said Harriet.
"Just keep reeling."

"It's so big, it will bite my hand off,"
yelled George.

"Here it comes," said Harriet.
"Ooops," said George.

"Better throw it back, George," said
Harriet. "It's too little to keep."

"Well, it felt big," said George.

Monday at school George told Ralph all
about the fishing trip.

"I caught a fish, and it was this big," he
said.

"How big, George?" said Harriet.
"Well, this big," said George.

"How big?"

"Well, maybe it was only this big," said George.

"But it sure put up a big fight!"